BEASTQUEST

⇥ BOOK TWELVE ⇤

TRILLION
THE THREE-HEADED LION

junior
Bla
8/12

ADAM BLADE
ILLUSTRATED BY EZRA TUCKER

SCHOLASTIC INC.
New York Toronto London Auckland Sydney
Mexico City New Delhi Hong Kong Buenos Aires

With special thanks to Allan Frewin

For Harvey

ISBN-13: 978-0-545-13266-4
ISBN-10: 0-545-13266-5

Beast Quest series created by Working Partners Ltd., London.
BEAST QUEST is a trademark of Working Partners Ltd.

Published by Scholastic Inc., 557 Broadway, New York, NY 10012, by arrangement with Working Partners Ltd.

12 11 10 9 8 7 6   11 12 13 14/0

Designed by Tim Hall
Printed in the U.S.A.
First printing, June 2009

Did you think it was over?

Did you think I would accept defeat and disappear?

No! That can never be. I am Malvel the Dark Wizard, who strikes fear into the hearts of the people of Avantia. I still have much more to show this wretched kingdom, and one boy in particular — Tom.

The young hero liberated the six Beasts of Avantia from my curse. But his fight is far from over. Let us see how he fares with a new Quest, one that will surely crush him and his companion, Elenna.

Avantia's Beasts had good hearts that I corrupted for my own wicked purpose. Now, thanks to Tom, they are free to protect the kingdom once more. But I have created new supreme Beasts whose hearts are evil and so cannot be set free. Each one guards a piece of the most precious relic of Avantia, a relic I have stolen: the suit of golden armor that gives magical strength to its rightful owner. I will stop at nothing to prevent Tom from collecting the complete suit and defeating me again. This time he will not win!

Malvel

THE SUN WAS SETTING OVER THE CENTRAL plains of Avantia. Tagus the Night Horse, good Beast and protector of the land, nodded contentedly. All was peaceful, as it had been ever since Tom had freed him from the evil curse of Malvel the Dark Wizard.

It was time to rest. The half-man, half-horse stamped a heavy hoof and turned to look at the cattle in the distance. A strange shape had appeared on an outcrop of rock on the far horizon, the sun behind it. Some kind of large animal was watching the herd.

A predator!

Tagus trotted forward warily, keeping to the cover of rocks and trees as he approached the creature. At last he was close enough to see clearly.

It was a huge three-headed lion, the last sunlight glinting on his thick golden fur and the shaggy manes that hung from his three heads. Six eyes burned with a wicked emerald light as he gazed down at the cattle, and his lips were drawn back to reveal fearsome, slavering teeth.

Tagus knew immediately that this was an evil Beast, sent by Malvel to cause mayhem. Instinct told him that he must confront the lion and do all in his power to destroy it. He eyed the huge paws, each one the size of his own head and studded with long, razor-sharp claws. Then, with a fierce cry, he galloped out of cover, puffing his chest as he pounded toward the lion.

The three heads turned and the three mouths bellowed with anger and hatred. The lion pounced from his position on the rock, filling the whole sky as he came crashing down on Tagus.

Tagus fought hard, kicking with his hooves and gripping one of the lion's three throats. But the two other heads came snapping at him and he could smell the Beast's foul breath as the three sets of teeth sought to tear his flesh from his bones.

A powerful double blow from Tagus's back legs sent the lion sprawling. Panting, the centaur got to his feet, but the evil Beast attacked again, jaws snapping, and his terrible weight bore him to the ground. Tagus had never known such strength and savagery. He could feel deep wounds on his flanks and neck, and sensed his death was near. The lion pinned him to the ground, his back arching as the three heads lifted and let out deafening, triumphant roars.

Tagus struggled valiantly, but he was already too weak to break free. The heads bent down now, hungry eyes glowing, jaws snapping and ready to sink into Tagus's flesh. . . .

Suddenly, an arrow came shooting out of

nowhere, the sharp point sinking deep into one of the lion's paws.

The monster let out a roar of anger and leaped back, his great body trembling with rage. Tagus tried to get up, but he was too badly wounded.

While one lion head tore at the arrow, the other two were turning, their blazing eyes searching for the archer. A second arrow hissed, narrowly missing one of the heads. With an earsplitting roar, the lion took off, bounding away toward the darkening plains.

Gasping with relief, Tagus looked up.

Two familiar shapes stood on the high horizon: a boy whose golden armor shone in the light of the setting sun, and a girl with another arrow already fitted to her bow. A horse and a wolf stood poised on the rocky outcrop behind them.

⇥ CHAPTER ONE ⇤

THE WOUNDED BEAST

"TAGUS IS HURT!" TOM CRIED, SCRAMBLING onto his horse. "Quickly, Storm!"

Elenna leaped up behind Tom. The black stallion neighed and reared, his hooves striking the air, before he set off at a gallop. Tom and Elenna clung grimly to his back, with Elenna's loyal wolf, Silver, close behind.

They came down off the stony crag and sped across the plains to where the injured Beast lay. Tagus was still struggling to get to his feet, but his battle with the monstrous three-headed lion had left him weak and helpless.

Tom peered into the distance, but the evil Beast

had fled, leaving no trace. There would be time enough to deal with Malvel's monster later. Right now they had to help Tagus.

"That lion would have killed Tagus if it wasn't for your arrows," Tom shouted to Elenna as they galloped along.

"It has to be one of Malvel's evil Beasts," Elenna replied, concern in her voice. "Do you think it's the guardian of the golden boots?"

"It must be," Tom said. "This is Malvel's final challenge — and when we win, I will have every piece of the missing golden armor."

The magical armor, the most precious relic in the kingdom, had been scattered throughout Avantia by the Dark Wizard, each piece watched over by a fearsome Beast under Malvel's thrall. So far, Tom had defeated five Beasts and collected the helmet, chain mail, breastplate, gauntlets, and leg armor. Each piece had given him new powers. Now only the boots were missing.

But Malvel had held back his most deadly Beast until last! The huge, savage creature had defeated Tagus — how could he and Elenna stand up to such a monster, even with the help of his magical shield and his golden armor?

Tom gritted his teeth. Whatever the outcome, he would defeat that Beast. The survival of the kingdom depended on it.

They came to where Tagus was lying. The foul, musky scent of the three-headed lion hung thickly in the air. The two friends leaped down from Storm's back and ran to Tagus. His wounds were deep and bloody, showing the dreadful marks of claws and of razor-sharp fangs.

"Careful!" Tom said as Tagus fought to get to his feet. "We'll help you. Slowly now!" The Beast could not understand human speech, but Tagus would know that they meant to help.

Tom and Elenna did their best to support

Tagus as he struggled to stand. Storm came close, whinnying gently and bowing his head so that Tagus could pull himself up.

At last the wounded Beast was upright, his arm across Storm's neck, the stallion pressing close so that Tagus would not fall. Silver prowled around them, his sharp eyes alert for danger.

"He needs to rest and recover," Elenna said, "but he won't be able to travel far." She looked at Tom. "What should we do?"

Tom pointed back toward the outcrop. The rock face curved inward, forming a natural place of shelter.

"If we can get him there, he should be hidden from danger while we deal with the lion," Tom said. He turned to Tagus. "Come with us," he said, pointing to the outcrop. "You'll be safe there."

The Beast nodded, his face twisted with pain.

Very slowly, and with Storm at his side, he began to limp forward.

Tom and Elenna walked at Tagus's other side, ready to help if the Night Horse faltered.

"He's badly hurt," Elenna said in a low voice. "He won't be able to help us against the lion."

Tom nodded grimly. In their Quest for the golden armor, they had been aided by the good Beasts of Avantia, but it seemed that this final test would have to be completed alone.

Then the sound of cruel laughter echoed across the plains.

"Malvel!" Tom gasped, his fingers closing on the hilt of his sword.

A dark swirl, like a small whirlwind, had appeared in the sky. When it cleared, the Dark Wizard was standing in front of them, his eyes flashing.

Tom drew his blade.

"Don't try to strike me," Malvel sneered. "You

know you cannot harm me!" He laughed again and stretched out a hand toward them, the long thin fingers like claws. "You are doomed. Your Quest is at an end! Tagus will die and you will fall to the power of Trillion — the most savage and deadly Beast you have ever encountered!"

"We're not scared of you or your Beasts!" Elenna shouted. "You're the one who should be scared!"

Malvel laughed. "Scared of you? No, child, I feel no fear. But fear is coming for you — can you not hear it? Padding this way on four mighty paws? Listen carefully now. . . ."

"You're a coward!" Tom shouted.

Malvel's face twisted with rage. "I will make you one oath, boy," he spat. "I promise you pain and destruction if you dare to fight Trillion. He is more dangerous than you could ever imagine!" His eyes glowed. "And when you lie dying, I will be there — and my face will be the last thing you will ever see!"

Then the dark whirlwind rose again, while the sky shook to the awful noise of the wizard's laughter.

Malvel was gone.

Tom turned to Elenna. "Aduro wasn't with him this time," he said.

Previously, Malvel had shown them horrible visions of their friend and adviser, the good wizard Aduro, bound and helpless above a pit of boiling tar. Tom knew that the only way to save Aduro was by collecting each piece of the golden armor and finishing the Quest.

"What do you think that means?" Elenna asked. "Has Malvel done something terrible to him?"

"I don't know," Tom replied, a new fierce determination in his voice. "But when this Quest is over, I will make Malvel pay for all his wickedness."

He gazed at the plains. Somewhere out there, Trillion was guarding the golden boots. Tom raised his sword to the sky.

"Whatever it takes," he called out, "I will find you, Trillion! I will complete my Quest!"

CHAPTER TWO

WILD ATTACK!

TAGUS LET OUT A GROAN. HE LAY ON THE ground underneath the outcrop, his great chest heaving and a trail of blood trickling from the corner of his mouth.

"I really think he's dying," Elenna whispered. "Tom — what can we do?"

"I have an idea!" Tom said. He pulled his shield off his back. Embedded in the wood were six magical tokens from his early Quests. "A phoenix can heal all wounds," he explained to Elenna as he pulled the feather of Epos the Winged Flame from its place in the shield. "Perhaps his token can help, too."

He knelt at Tagus's side and touched the feather against one of the Beast's deep cuts. A sudden surge of energy filled his hand and shot up his arm, making his skin tingle, and the feather began to glow red.

"It's working!" Elenna gasped.

"I think it is," Tom agreed with a smile. He lifted the token away. The wound had closed, hardly leaving a scar. "But there are so many injuries," he murmured. "I wonder if it will have enough power to heal them all."

He put the feather to another wound. Again he felt the tingling sensation and again the red light surged. Hope ignited in him — soon Tagus would be well again!

But when he tried to heal the third wound, the tingling was faint and the light barely gleamed. Tom lifted the feather away. The wound had closed, but it hadn't completely healed.

Tom touched a fourth wound. The light flickered for a moment, then it was gone.

"Why isn't it working?" Elenna asked.

"I think it needs time to fill with power again," Tom said. He looked anxiously at her. "At least, I hope that's all it is." He frowned. "But it might take hours or days, for all we know. And we don't have that kind of time!" He stood up, gripping the feather. "We have to act against Trillion now," he said. "The evil Beast can't be allowed to ravage the countryside." He pointed to the top of the rock that was sheltering them. "That's a good vantage point," he said. "I should be able to see Trillion if he's anywhere nearby."

"I'll come with you," Elenna said. "Storm and Silver can stay with Tagus."

Tom nodded. He and Elenna said a quick farewell to their two companions, then began the steep climb to the summit of the outcrop.

The sun had set by the time they stood on the

high rock. Tom lowered the visor of his golden helmet, which gave him brilliant vision.

Now Tom could see the three-headed lion as clearly as if the Beast had been a sword's length away.

Trillion was causing havoc in a herd of wild goats, leaping upon the terrified, fleeing creatures. The poor animals were snapped up in the lion's jaws, then flung away.

"He's toying with them!" Tom said angrily, his heart burning. "We'll put a stop to his game!"

But Elenna snatched at his arm. "Look!"

Tom followed the line of her eyes. A wide ring of small dark shapes was moving purposefully in their direction.

"Hyenas!" he gasped. There were twenty or thirty of them, slinking toward Tagus, Storm, and Silver, their eyes shining with a hungry light.

"They must have smelled Tagus's blood," Tom said.

"Will Storm and Silver be able to fight them off?" Elenna asked anxiously.

"I don't think so," Tom said. "There are too many of them. We have to get back down there."

A drawn-out howl sounded from one of the hyenas, and then the entire pack came forward at a run, screeching and yowling as they closed in on the helpless Beast and his two animal protectors. . . .

CHAPTER THREE

COURAGE AND STRENGTH

"WE'RE COMING!" TOM SHOUTED AS HE AND Elenna scrambled back down the rock face. They were soon nearly at the bottom.

But the hyenas were closing in fast, their howling echoing across the plains.

"I left my bow and arrows down there," Elenna cried.

Tom held out his shield. "Use this to defend yourself while you get them," he said.

"But you'll need it!" Elenna gasped.

"I have other protection," Tom replied, his hand pressing against his chain mail and shining breastplate. The moment his hand touched the golden armor, he felt the magic working. The chain mail filled his heart with blazing courage. At the same time, he felt strength flowing from the breastplate to all his muscles.

He felt no fear now. A thousand hyenas could attack — he would defeat them! He pressed the shield into Elenna's hands and leaped from the rock with a shout, his sword flashing in his hand.

He landed among the hyenas, his blade slicing the air, his other arm raised to fend off the gnashing teeth and scrabbling claws. A few hyenas fell and the others drew back, surrounding him, glaring at him, but keeping out of sword's reach.

He saw Elenna leap down off the rock, the shield held out in front of her. A hyena pounced, but she struck it with the shield and sent it tumbling.

"You won't defeat me!" Elenna cried out to the vicious animals. Another hyena came at her, but she sidestepped and kicked out as it plunged past her.

Storm and Silver were also fighting hard, battling to keep the hyenas away from Tagus. Storm was rearing, beating the hyenas back with his kicking hooves, the power of his legs sending the wild animals spinning through the air. Tagus was trying to get to his feet, but Tom could see he was weak from loss of blood and could do nothing to help.

Silver was on the ground, wrestling wildly with two of the hyenas. For a dreadful moment, one of the hyenas managed to clamp its jaws to the wolf's neck, but Silver quickly struggled to his feet, shaking off his attacker.

Swinging his sword, Tom ran forward. "Storm! To me!" he shouted.

The noble stallion neighed loudly at the sound of his voice and came plunging toward him through the mass of hyenas, hooves stamping.

Tom swung up into the saddle, grasping the reins and urging Storm toward the wolf and the night horse. His blade flashed and spun, the golden gauntlets bestowing special sword skills. The cowardly hyenas backed away, snarling and slavering, as Tom reached Silver. A moment later and Elenna was at his side, her bowstring thrumming as she shot arrow after arrow into the pack.

"Get away!" Tom shouted at the remaining hyenas.

A long, whining howl of defeat sounded. The pack slunk back, then turned and fled. Filled with joy, Tom dug his heels into Storm's flanks, urging the horse to gallop after them. He wasn't going to let them regroup and attack again — he would give them such a chase that they would never come back!

Elenna shouted, "Tom, be careful!"

But he had no fear.

Suddenly, a howl sounded from the rocks on one side. He turned his head and saw a huge hyena standing above him. Then there was another howl — from the other side. He turned his head again and saw the shapes of more hyenas.

Two new packs had arrived!

Storm whinnied uneasily, turning about as the packs swarmed closer. They began to screech again, and this time there was a new hunger in their eyes.

Tom raised his sword as the hyenas pounced.

⇥ CHAPTER FOUR ⇤

THE FEATHER OF EPOS

A ROAR SOUNDED IN THE GATHERING twilight, a roar so loud it shook the air. The high-pitched baying of the hyenas was silenced.

Tom twisted in the saddle.

Tagus was approaching! The centaur had come to save him!

The good Beast was bloodied and his hide was crisscrossed with cuts, but he was standing tall and majestic again, his head held high, his great hooves stamping and his sword in his fist.

A few hyenas threw themselves at the Beast, but each of his massive hooves sliced through the air like a scythe as he thundered into the pack and scattered the animals.

"Tagus!" Tom shouted in joy, brandishing his sword.

The hyenas turned tail, racing into the gathering gloom.

Tom rode up to Tagus. "You made it just in time," he said, hoping the Beast would understand what he was trying to say.

Tagus nodded his huge head and there was a proud light in his eyes. But he was panting and his efforts had opened his wounds again, so that the blood splashed onto the ground.

As Elenna and Silver came running, Tagus staggered, his legs giving way beneath him. Tom let out a cry of concern as the good Beast collapsed to the ground.

"It was too much for him," said Elenna, resting her hand gently on Tagus's neck.

"He used all his strength to save us," Tom said anxiously, swinging down from the saddle and running to Tagus's side. "Elenna — give me the shield, please. Maybe Epos's feather will work again now."

Tagus lay quite still, breathing heavily, his eyes half closed as Tom placed the feather against the worst of the wounds. The tingle ran up his arm and the red light glowed. "It's working!" Tom cried in relief.

While Tom concentrated on the next wound, Elenna gathered moss to clean Tagus's injuries and to soak up the blood. Storm whinnied softly, touching his velvet muzzle comfortingly to the side of the Night Horse's face. Even Silver came and curled up at the Beast's side to keep Tagus warm as the last light of day dwindled.

"How long will Epos's feather work?" asked Elenna.

Tom looked up at her. "Long enough to save him from dying, I hope," he said. A few wounds had been healed, but there were so many more.

"It only has the power to heal a few wounds at a time," Elenna pointed out. "It could take all night."

"Then we *will* take all night," Tom said firmly. "I'm not leaving him like this, not after what he did for us. Besides, I think we should rest after our fight with the hyenas. We'll need all our wits and strength before we try to tackle Trillion."

A roar sounded in the distance. Tom looked up. The three-headed lion stood on a hilltop, silhouetted against the rising moon.

"Why doesn't he attack?" Elenna asked.

"He's hoping to lure us into chasing him in the darkness," Tom said, his eyes narrowing. "He probably has a trap planned for us."

At that moment, Trillion leaped down from the hilltop and vanished into the night.

Elenna stared after him. "By morning, he could be a long way from here!" she exclaimed. "We could lose him."

"He won't get away," Tom declared. "Aduro's enchanted map will guide us to him." He drew out the rolled-up parchment map from Storm's saddlebag and flung it open.

Tom had been given the magical map of Avantia at the very beginning of his Quest. Rolled up, it seemed to be an ordinary map, but when it was laid flat, something extraordinary happened — it turned into a tiny living version of the kingdom, with rivers that ran and treetops that swayed gently in the breeze. The map had always shown Tom the path to the next Beast.

Tom and Elenna stared at the map and waited. But there was no sign of Trillion on the miniature parchment plains.

"How can we fight a Beast we can't find?" Elenna said.

"I don't know," Tom said. "But there *has* to be a way!"

Just then Silver got up and began to bark. He trotted away from them, his nose to the ground. Then he turned and came back to Tom and Elenna, barking again and nudging his gray head against Tom's arm. The moonlight reflected brightly in his eager eyes.

"What is it, boy?" Tom asked.

Silver sniffed again and pawed the ground, looking at Tom and Elenna, then stared off into the distance.

A smile broke over Elenna's face. "He's telling us we don't need the map," she said. "He'll use his nose to track Trillion down." She grinned at Tom. "A wolf can do more than just fight!"

"Well done, Silver!" said Tom. "We'll stay

here with Tagus overnight, and first thing in the morning you can lead us to Trillion." He patted the wolf's thick fur. "I *will* defeat him, and then the golden armor will be complete!"

→ CHAPTER FIVE ←

HUNTER AND PREY

THE SUN HAD JUST STARTED TO RISE OVER THE hills the next morning when Silver leaped onto a rock and sniffed the air. He let out a growl and bounded away. Tom and Elenna bid farewell to Tagus, who was now well enough to stand. Then Tom jumped into Storm's saddle, reaching down to help Elenna climb up behind him.

Storm took off after the racing wolf, Tom and Elenna clinging to his back.

"From the way Silver is behaving, I don't think Trillion can be very far away," Elenna said as they galloped over the plains.

"He isn't!" Tom said. "Can't you smell him?"

The foul smell of the three-headed Beast filled the air. Then the wind changed direction and Tom lost the scent. But Silver's sensitive wolf nose did not let them down. His muzzle to the ground, his tail waving high in the air, he led them toward a distant ridge.

Sometime later they approached the top of the ridge. Silver paused.

"I think he wants us to hold back," Elenna said.

They waited while the wolf crept to the crest. Keeping low, he peered over, then came loping back, his tongue lolling and his eyes filled with triumph.

"I think Trillion is just beyond the ridge," Elenna whispered. "Well done, Silver!"

Tom and Elenna dismounted and crawled up to the crest. They found themselves looking down into a wide forested valley, which sloped down to a lake of still water that glimmered in the sunlight.

Tall fir trees grew right up to the water's edge, but in one place there was a clearing. Trillion was pacing slowly along the shore. A thrill of excitement ran through Tom. There could only be one reason why Trillion was here — the golden boots! The Quest was almost over, though he knew it would take all his courage and cunning to defeat the Beast.

"He's so big," Elenna murmured. "Tom, how will we ever beat him?"

Tom frowned. "He must have a weak spot," he said, and lowered his visor, so that he could study every detail of the giant lion. As Tom watched, a bird came swooping low over the water and Trillion lunged toward it, teeth bared and one paw swiping. The bird gave a cry of alarm and rocketed up into the sky. But Tom noticed that Trillion's other paw came close to the water's edge and that the evil Beast quickly drew back with a snarl.

"I've heard stories that lions are afraid of

water," Tom said. "They aren't good swimmers, because their manes get waterlogged and drag them down."

"And Trillion has *three* manes," Elenna said. "If we can lure him into the lake, we might be able to defeat him!"

Tom watched the lion, a plan forming in his mind.

"Storm isn't afraid of water," he said. "He's swum rivers with me on his back. If we could get him to go down to the lakeside to drink, I'm sure he would lure the lion."

Elenna stared at him with wide, frightened eyes. "You can't mean it!" she gasped. "Trillion could kill Storm with one bite!"

"I know," Tom admitted. "It's dangerous, but I can't think of any other way to take Trillion by surprise." He looked back to where the stallion stood waiting. "Storm is clever," he said. "When he sees the lion coming for him, he will leap into the water and swim to safety. We'll wait in hiding nearby. As soon as the lion gets to the water's edge, you can fire arrows at him, I'll attack with my sword, and with luck we'll force him into the lake."

"And if we don't have any luck?" Elenna murmured.

"Then I will do everything in my power to see that Storm does not come to harm!" Tom vowed.

"You're right," Elenna said. "What other choice is there?"

They found a low place in the ridge and made their way down through the trees, moving silently. Tom led Storm, keeping close to him, rubbing his face against the animal's neck.

"I wish I could spare you this danger," he said to the black stallion.

Storm whinnied softly, almost as if he knew what Tom was going to ask him to do. Tom wondered if his lost father, Taladon the Swift, had ever had to face such a heart-wrenching decision.

At last they came down to where the trees met the lake's edge. Trillion's clearing was to their left. Tom peered through the trees. The lion had left the clearing, but Tom thought he saw a glimpse of tawny fur at the far edge of the open space.

Tom stroked Storm's neck. "Go, boy," he said. "Have a drink." He knew Storm couldn't understand his words, but he added, "The moment you see the lion, jump into the water and swim away as fast as you can. We'll do the rest." He just had to hope Storm would know what to do.

Storm pressed his muzzle into Tom's neck.

As the brave horse walked out of the cover of the trees and trotted down to the edge of the lake, Tom drew his sword and Elenna fitted an arrow to her bow.

"We may be too far away," Tom said. "Follow me." He led Elenna and Silver to a place close to the middle of the clearing. Now they were in a much better position to attack the lion.

Tom stared into the trees, carefully keeping watch on the last place he thought he had seen Trillion. He could see no sign of the Beast now — but was sure he must be lurking nearby. The foul smell still filled the air.

Storm lowered his head and began to drink. Tom's heart was thumping. He mustn't let anything happen to his horse.

Still the lion did not come. Where was Trillion?

"Oh no!" Elenna gasped. "Look!"

Tom turned at the sound of her voice, and his heart leaped into his mouth.

Trillion was on the *other* side of the clearing! He must have gone right around the lake under cover of the trees, and was coming at Storm from behind!

The evil Beast slunk silently out of the trees, his body low to the ground, his eyes fixed on Tom's black stallion.

A terrible panic gripped Tom. Storm was too far away for them to reach him in time! And he couldn't call out to warn the horse because that would let Trillion know where they were.

The plan had gone horribly wrong.

↦ CHAPTER SIX ↤

DESPERATE DANGER!

Tom scrambled to his feet, but Elenna snatched at his arm and pulled him down again.

"It's too late. Trillion will see you!" she hissed. "Keep under the cover of the trees, make your way behind him — then attack. As soon as you make your move, I'll start shooting arrows."

Tom nodded. "Good thinking," he said. But there was so little time. He could see that Trillion was getting terribly close to Storm, and still the horse had not heard him.

Tom slid quietly along the edge of the forest until he was behind the great three-headed lion. He could see the monster's huge paw prints in the soft earth — each as large as Tom's shield. Trillion was the most dangerous Beast he had ever faced. The courage bestowed by the golden chain mail was barely enough, but Tom knew what he had to do. He took a step out into the open and raised his arm to give Elenna the signal to begin firing her arrows.

As the first arrow bit into the Beast's shoulder, Trillion let out a fearsome roar from all three of his massive jaws, an earsplitting noise that sent birds wheeling into the sky. Storm's head jerked up and he rolled his eyes in fear, rearing back from the huge Beast. But instead of leaping forward into the safety of the lake, Storm bolted for the trees.

"No, Storm!" Tom shouted. "Not that way!"

Trillion was too quick for the horse. Ignoring the arrow that jutted from his thick hide, the lion pounced, blocking Storm's escape route. Tom saw his friend rear up in panic, froth gathering at the corners of his mouth.

Storm turned on his hind legs and raced for the lake, but in three great bounds, Trillion was between the horse and the water, wicked eyes glinting and jaws gaping as he snarled and pawed the ground. It seemed to Tom that the Beast was enjoying tormenting Storm — as if killing Tom's horse would be a special pleasure.

Trillion raised a paw, claws extended, ready to deliver the killing blow. But a second arrow flew from the forest. It struck Trillion in the hindquarters and hung there, quivering. Tom saw Elenna step out of the trees, already fitting an arrow to her bow. The lion roared. Elenna fired again. The arrow hissed through the air, catching in one of Trillion's manes. Another struck him, and then another — but they didn't seem to be injuring Trillion at all. Tom realized that the lion's hide must be too thick for the arrows to penetrate.

Storm was standing his ground even though he

was terrified. Tom knew that once the horse ran, Trillion would bring him down.

He had to act fast. It was time to break his cover — to rescue Storm and defeat Trillion.

Another arrow came arcing out of the trees. But this time flames were crackling around its point! Elenna must have tied dry grasses around the arrowhead, then used flint and tinder to ignite it. Fire arrows were her specialty.

"Yes!" Tom whispered to himself. "Good for you, Elenna."

The arrow embedded itself in Trillion's foreleg, the flames searing the Beast's hair and burning his skin. Trillion let out a roar of pain, twisting and turning as he tried to quench the flames.

Tom knew this was his chance. He ran forward, quickly covering the open ground between himself and Storm, his golden leg armor giving him the extra speed that he needed. He was nearly there! Trillion pulled the arrow from his flesh with his teeth, ignoring the flames. But the Beast froze when he saw Tom grab Storm's leather reins.

Another deafening roar blared from Trillion's three gaping mouths. Storm bolted, heading toward the water, with Tom clinging to the reins. The golden armor clattered as he was dragged along and his sword fell from his fingers.

Tom lost his grip on the reins when Storm plunged into the lake. The water closed over his head and flooded his mouth. The golden armor was dragging him down. Tom kicked hard with his feet and hauled himself up to the surface, coughing and spluttering. If it hadn't been for the protection of Sepron the Sea Serpent's tooth on his shield, he would certainly have drowned!

Trillion was now at the lake's edge. The Beast didn't dare come into the water but reached out a giant paw toward Storm. The fearsome claws caught Storm's saddle. With one swift movement, the stallion was plucked from the lake and sent rolling onto the ground, his long legs kicking in the air.

More arrows flew from the forest. But they were no help. Tom had to get back to shore! He swam as fast as he could, kicking fiercely to stay afloat. He grabbed hold of some reeds and hauled himself onto dry land. Struggling to his feet, he ran toward Storm. But he was too late. Trillion leaped at the horse, his claws glinting in the sun.

Then, with a sudden shock, Tom saw the sunlight reflecting off something else — the golden boots! They were lying half hidden in the long grass, close to the fallen stallion.

As Trillion came plunging down, Tom realized that the Beast was going to crush both Storm and the magical boots.

"No!" Tom cried out. "Storm!"

CHAPTER SEVEN

THE LION'S BREATH

AT THE LAST POSSIBLE MOMENT, STORM managed to roll clear of Trillion. His kicking legs struck the golden boots with a clang and sent them spinning to safety. The huge lion crashed to the ground, tumbling over and over. Storm managed to scramble up and race toward Tom, whinnying loudly.

"Well done, boy!" Tom shouted.

The water gushing from his golden armor, Tom stooped to pick up his fallen sword. Storm was close now, still moving at great speed. Using the power of his leg armor, Tom ran alongside his

horse, easily keeping pace with him. He snatched at Storm's reins and swung himself up into the saddle, using the strength given to him by the golden breastplate to mount the stallion at a gallop.

"To Elenna!" he shouted.

Storm turned and reared, neighing loudly. Moments later he was galloping toward the protection of the trees where Elenna and Silver were waiting.

But Trillion was on his feet again, letting out roar after enraged roar. Tom looked back over his shoulder and saw a deadly light in the lion's fierce green eyes. The evil Beast was getting ready for the kill.

Tom leaned into the wind as Storm raced frantically for the trees.

"Come on!" he called. "Faster, Storm!"

The lion was suddenly horribly close, and Tom could feel that hot, foul breath on his neck. The

Beast's jaws snapped, and Storm sidestepped, giving them a few desperate moments while the lion changed direction to keep after them — but it also meant they were now heading away from the trees again.

Storm made another sudden change of direction, but Trillion was ready for it this time and his claws slashed through the air, nearly tearing Tom from the saddle. One of the huge heads came terrifyingly close, the open mouth red, the teeth slavering.

Tom kicked out, shouting, "Keep going, Storm! Don't give up!" But he misjudged the kick, and Trillion's fangs closed around his ankle.

Tom let out a cry of pain as the teeth clamped down and Trillion tried to wrench him from Storm. Tom swung his sword at the Beast, but he was using so much of his strength to stay in the saddle that his blow went wild. Before he could gather himself to strike again, Trillion bit down on Tom's leg and shook him violently. Tom's fingers were ripped from the reins and he fell with a shout.

He struck the ground hard, only his armor saving him from breaking bones. He lost hold of his sword and shield, but a shred of luck was with him as he rolled over and over, his armor clanking and rattling. His leg was free of Trillion's grasp!

The shooting pains in his leg were intense. He tried to get to his feet, but his ankle gave way under him and he sprawled breathlessly on the ground. He could see Elenna and Silver running toward him from the trees.

"No!" he cried. "Go back!" He spotted his sword and shield nearby, and began desperately to crawl toward them.

His fingers were about to close around the hilt of his sword when a massive shape came bounding toward him. Two huge paws came crashing down on the sword and the shield. Tom looked up.

Trillion's three heads reared above him, the six green eyes filled with malice. A blast of stinking breath almost choked Tom as the heads lowered, the drooling jaws ready to rip him to pieces.

The Quest was lost!

→ CHAPTER EIGHT ←

THE GOOD BEAST

WITH A ROAR, TRILLION BROUGHT HIS PAW down on Tom's breastplate. Tom gasped as he felt the weight of the lion bearing down on him, pressing him into the ground.

But the golden armor held!

The three heads came closer, a paw swiping across Tom's face. His helmet saved him from serious injury, but his visor was up and the points of the monster's claws sliced the skin of his cheek, drawing blood.

The middle head loomed closer, jaws gaping.

Then Tom heard galloping hooves.

His horse was coming to the rescue. But Tom knew that Storm was no match for Trillion.

"Go back!" he shouted.

A howl of rage answered him.

Tom twisted around, still pinned to the ground by the evil Beast, and saw with astonishment that it wasn't Storm.

It was *Tagus*!

The good Beast was galloping across the clearing, his eyes flashing as he bore down on the three-headed lion.

Tagus struck Trillion like an avalanche, kicking, bellowing war cries, and driving forward with incredible ferocity.

Gasping for breath, Tom managed to roll clear of the two Beasts. Trillion was roaring with pain and fury, and rose up, his claws like knives, lunging at the centaur. But Tagus turned in a moment, bringing his hindquarters forward and lashing out

with a powerful double kick that sent Trillion staggering backward.

Tom saw what Tagus was doing. He shouted to Elenna, "He's driving Trillion toward the lake! We have to help!"

Tom got to his feet, ignoring the pain in his ankle as he stumbled to snatch up his sword. He limped forward, ready to join battle with Tagus. Thrusting his blade, he slashed at the lion's forelegs, helping to force Trillion closer and closer to the water's edge.

"I'm coming!" Tom heard Elenna shout. Out of the corner of his eye, he saw Storm gallop up with Elenna on his back and Silver loping at his side. Elenna leaned far out of the saddle and snatched up Tom's shield, throwing it to him as Storm raced past.

"Thank you!" Tom caught the shield gratefully, but the pain in his ankle was so bad that he could barely stand.

"I will not give up!" he hissed under his breath, his sword stabbing and cutting at the lion, his shield defending him from the evil Beast's ripping claws. "While there is blood in my veins, I will fight on!"

He shouted to Elenna, trying to lift his voice against the noise of the battling Beasts. "Keep back — all of you! Don't let Storm get too close!" He was not going to risk the horse's life a second time. And there was something vitally important that he wanted Elenna and Storm to do. "I've seen the boots!" Tom yelled. "They're lying over there, in the grass!"

"I see them!" Elenna shouted back. "We'll get them for you!"

Hope filled Tom's heart — but while he was distracted, a paw struck him, knocking him to the ground. Shaking his head, he got to his feet, but the fall had made his injured ankle worse; he could hardly put any weight on it now.

"You're hurt!" Elenna cried. "I'll get you to safety first!"

"No!" Tom shouted, his voice rising above the roaring of the Beasts. "I'm fine — and I won't leave Tagus. Rescue the boots!"

Elenna hesitated, then pulled on Storm's reins, turning the horse. With Silver close behind, she raced toward the boots.

Tom turned again to the desperate battle, hoping he could survive the pain in his ankle long enough to defeat the lion. But with every step toward the lake, Trillion fought more fiercely, and Tagus was beginning to tire.

Suddenly, Tom's ankle gave way; he fell to his knees. He needed to be brave as never before. He looked up at Trillion and saw him take another deadly swipe at Tagus. *Enough!* Tom touched his hand against the golden chain mail, which would give him strength of heart. Slowly, he clambered back to his feet, gritting his teeth as he tried to ignore the pain. Finally, he drew himself up to his full height and raised his sword in the air.

He was ready to end the battle with Trillion.

CHAPTER NINE

NO VICTORY!

THE TWO BEASTS WERE STILL FIGHTING furiously. The lake was only a short distance away, but driving the three-headed lion back those last few paces was going to take every ounce of strength and courage Tom possessed.

"I'm coming!" he shouted, hobbling forward, knowing that he was facing a Beast more evil and vicious than any he had encountered before.

Tagus bellowed as his hooves struck the lion again and again, but the pounding force was barely able to penetrate the evil Beast's thick hide. With every blow, Tom could see that Tagus was weakening — and the fangs in those three snarling mouths were as sharp and dangerous as ever.

It was now or never! Tom darted toward the lion, coming in behind the three heads, aiming for the huge body. Gripping his sword in both hands, he lunged forward.

The blade sank deep into the fur and flesh. One of the heads turned angrily and Tom threw himself to the ground as a great paw swung toward his head. His sword blow had not injured the lion, merely angered him.

What kind of Beast is this? Tom thought. Nothing seemed to hurt him. How could he ever be defeated?

The massive paw struck Tom a glancing blow on the head. He rolled over, dizzy and half stunned.

Tagus bellowed and grunted as he struggled to beat the lion back.

Then Tom saw a shape looming above him. He

blinked, trying to focus. It was Storm. Elenna was in the saddle and Silver by their side, and Elenna was carrying something that gleamed and shone in the sunlight.

The golden boots!

Tom sat up, his head still spinning.

Elenna leaped from the saddle, holding the boots out. "Put them on!" she said.

He reached out, but he was dazed and could barely see straight.

"You'll have to put them on my feet," he gasped. "Quickly! Tagus won't last much longer."

Elenna knelt down and pushed the golden boots onto Tom's feet, taking care with his injured ankle.

Tom sat, panting and giddy, waiting for some sign that the boots would make a difference.

"How do you feel?" Elenna asked anxiously. "Can you stand?"

"No," Tom gasped. Why weren't the boots

helping him? Was the Quest going to fail at the final moment?

But then a tingling began to course through him, bringing with it a sensation of strength and power that seemed to flow through his veins. The pain in his ankle faded, and suddenly he was clearheaded again.

He sprang to his feet. He felt he could leap over the treetops. This was the power of the golden boots! Gripping his sword and shield, he ran toward the battling Beasts. Trillion's last moment had come. Nothing could save the lion now.

Tom lifted his sword, ready to deliver the final blow. But a few paces away from Trillion, he was brought to a halt by an invisible force. He staggered back, then ran forward once more. Again the invisible wall repelled him. He could not get to the evil Beast.

What was happening?

A black whirlwind appeared close to the water's edge. The air was shrill with the howling wind, but then the darkness was gone — and Malvel was standing at the lakeside.

The Dark Wizard was keeping Tom from the monster! Tom beat at the invisible wall with his sword, but he could not get through.

"I warn you, boy — if you achieve victory here, you will regret it!" Malvel called. "It will take you to places you would not choose to visit."

Tom felt the power of Avantia blazing in him. "I don't care!" he shouted, hacking at the wall. "I will defeat you, Malvel — whatever the price!"

"Such arrogance in one so young!" Malvel cried.

He made a wide gesture with his arm, and suddenly an image of Aduro appeared. Tom gasped. The good wizard was lying on the ground, beaten and bloodied.

Behind Malvel's invisible barrier, Tagus and

Trillion were still fighting furiously. Silver was scrabbling against the barrier, howling with anger and frustration. Elenna was firing arrows from Storm's back, but the arrows were bouncing uselessly off the magical force field.

"I warn you one last time," cried Malvel. "If you defeat Trillion, I will make you pay in ways that you cannot imagine!"

Tom let his sword arm fall as he stared at the image of his good friend. Aduro was a powerful wizard, and yet Malvel had crushed him. How could Tom hope to stand against such evil strength?

CHAPTER TEN

THE LION GATE

A TRIUMPHANT ROAR FROM TRILLION MADE
Tom turn away from the Dark Wizard. Tagus was
falling back, his strength failing. The great lion
was overpowering him. The battle would soon
be lost.

"Remember my words!" Malvel called.

"I shall," Tom shouted defiantly. "But they
won't stop me!"

His sword wasn't able to break through the
invisible wall, but he felt more power rising up
through his body, power that was coming from
the golden boots. Could they destroy the magical
barrier?

He brought one foot back and then let fly with a powerful kick. There was a noise so loud that it sounded like the sky shattering. Malvel let out a howl of rage. The invisible barrier was gone!

Tom ran forward. But suddenly, both sword and shield flew from his grip. Malvel was stopping at nothing!

"Tom! No — get back!" Elenna called. "You'll be killed."

"I don't need any weapons," Tom shouted, his whole body tingling with energy. "My armor gives me all the strength I need!"

Tagus was down, still kicking, as the evil Beast loomed over him. Tom leaped at the lion, grabbing one of his manes. Digging his heels into Trillion's shoulders, he heaved backward.

Trillion stumbled to one side, taken by surprise by Tom's assault, but turned his head quickly, the jaws opening. Undaunted, Tom thrust his arm into the lion's mouth. The golden armor held! Tom saw the lion's teeth splintering into shards.

With a roar of agony, the head reared back, blood dripping from the foaming lips, and the lion dropped onto his haunches. All three heads pulled away from Tom, the six green eyes filled with pain, and one of Trillion's huge paws shot toward Tom with claws unsheathed. Tom knocked the paw aside with a single blow of his fist. Trillion roared again and a vicious light ignited in his eyes. Rearing up, he prepared to bring all his mighty weight down on Tom and crush him to the ground.

But as Trillion lifted himself onto his hind legs, Tom saw his opportunity. Instead of running away from the Beast, he lunged forward, his arms up above his head, pushing against Trillion's underbelly. The armor had made him so powerful that he was able to force the lion backward.

"I'm stronger than you now!" Tom shouted. "You've failed!"

Roaring and snarling, Trillion fell back, his claws useless, his three sets of teeth biting on the air. Again and again, Tom pushed, driving the Beast closer to the lake. He had never been so determined.

Too late, the evil Beast realized his peril. Trillion tried to writhe away, to avoid the water, but Tom was merciless. With a final mighty shove, he sent the lion plunging into the lake.

The water foamed as the Beast thrashed helplessly. But the more Trillion struggled, the deeper he sank, his thick fur becoming waterlogged, his great manes dragging him down.

Tom stood at the water's edge, unable to tear his eyes away from the dreadful sight as the lion fought to keep afloat. There was terror and fury in the six green eyes as the waters closed over the three heads. A paw broke the surface for a moment, then Trillion was gone. Bubbles boiled, followed by a strange hush. The roaring of the three-headed lion was silenced forever.

Elenna stood at Tom's side. She rested her hand on his shoulder.

"You did it," she said quietly. "You defeated the most powerful Beast Malvel has ever sent!"

But Tom frowned. All the evil Beasts he had fought in his Quest for the golden armor had dissolved into small versions of themselves after he had vanquished them. He was expecting the same to happen with Trillion. But the lake's surface was clear and smooth. He looked at Elenna. "There aren't any little lions," he said. "Why do you think that is?"

"I don't know," Elenna said. "Perhaps . . ."

Her words were interrupted by a low rumbling sound that made the ground tremble under their feet. The surface of the lake began to shiver.

Ripples spread from the place where Trillion had last been seen. The water surged and heaved, and a deep growl shook the air.

Then the waters parted as a vast domed shape rose majestically out of the lake, black as ebony, running with water, shining darkly in the sun. It towered above the two friends, shedding rivers of lake water.

A statue of a huge lion's head stood before them, its jaws wide open. A causeway had formed between it and the shore, and a path led through the enormous teeth.

"It's a gateway," Tom murmured in awe.

"Leading where?" Elenna murmured.

"I don't know," Tom replied. "But I have to follow the path. Something is drawing me forward."

"It could be dangerous," Elenna warned. "Malvel may have created it."

Tom looked back. The Dark Wizard had

vanished. "That doesn't matter," he said. He took his magical compass from his pocket and held it out in front of him. It had been left to him by his father, Taladon, and had already saved his life. The needle pointed to Destiny.

A powerful certainty filled Tom. "I know where Malvel has gone," he said. He pointed to the open jaws. "He's beyond the gateway. And I think Aduro is there, too." He looked at Elenna. "I have to go."

"You mean *we* have to go," Elenna said.

Tom turned and saw that Storm and Silver were right behind them. Not for the first time, he was grateful to have such loyal friends.

Tom took Storm's reins and strode out onto the causeway, his horse following fearlessly. Elenna walked at his shoulder, her hand in Silver's gray fur as he paced alongside her.

The air shimmered all around the lion's jaws, tingling on Tom's skin and making his hair stand on end. As the four companions paused before the gaping fangs, Tom's golden armor glowed in the sunlight.

He and Elenna exchanged glances.

"Ready?" Tom asked.

"Ready," Elenna reassured him.

Then the four friends walked into the lion's gate, following the path that would lead them to their next adventure.

Tom had a destiny to fulfill. The Quest was far from over.

THE SECRETS OF DROON

By Tony Abbott

Under the stairs, a magical world awaits you!

■ SCHOLASTIC

www.scholastic.com/droon

DROO